Horace Hills Morgan

Representative names in the history of English literature

Horace Hills Morgan

Representative names in the history of English literature

ISBN/EAN: 9783744748902

Printed in Europe, USA, Canada, Australia, Japan

Cover: Foto ©Andreas Hilbeck / pixelio.de

More available books at **www.hansebooks.com**

REPRESENTATIVE NAMES

IN THE HISTORY OF

ENGLISH LITERATURE

———

BY H. H. MORGAN

———

NEW YORK:

D. APPLETON AND COMPANY,

549 AND 551 BROADWAY.

1876.

DEDICATED

TO

THOSE WHO FEEL THE NECESSITY

FOR A

Wider Diffusion of the Results attained by Students,

AND

SEEKING THE APPROVAL OF THOSE WHO,

BY THEIR

Acquaintance with Literature,

ARE

RENDERED COMPETENT TO EXPRESS

A

Rational Opinion.

PREFACE.

The wants of a busy age require some inexpensive book which shall furnish general information, together with a firm grasp of the movement in each field of effort. As auxiliary to our anthologies, dictionaries of authors, bibliographies, and manuals of literature, it has seemed not undesirable to have some "vade mecum" in which should be collected information otherwise accessible only by long and continuous labor. The plan adopted aims at an answer to the various rational questions which might be asked about an author as an author: when did he live, who were his contemporaries, what was his standpoint, what are his representative works, for what and how far can we trust him, who vouched for his reliability, and what did he do to further the progress of literature?

The selection of names has been made with reference to the authors whom the world has accepted as representative of English literature; as minor writers there have been added those whose services have an historical value. Literature has been understood in the strictest sense—the perfect adaptation of the form to the thought expressed; judgment is pronounced from the æsthetic point of view, and not from that of Ethics, Politics, or Commerce; Oratory, Theology, Physics, and Metaphysics have been excluded except when their form has entitled them to literary recognition.

The time of any author has been indicated by giving the date of his birth and death, together with the "Era" in which he would be classed. The classification of Wm. Francis Collier is noticeably simple and serviceable, and has been used; it is as follows:—

ist Era. From the birth of Chaucer, 1328, to the Introduction of Printing, 1474.
iid " " " Introduction of Printing, 1474, to the accession of Elizabeth, 1558.
iiid " " " Accession of Elizabeth, 1558, to the shutting of the Theatres, 1648.
ivth " " " Shutting of the Theatres, 1648, to the Death of Milton, 1674.
vth " " " Death of Milton, 1674, to the Publication of the Tatler, 1709.
vith " " " Publication of the Tatler, 1709, to the Publication of Pamela, 1740.
viith Era. " " " . " Pamela, 1740, to the Death of Johnson, 1784.
viiith " " " Death of Johnson, 1784, to the Death of Scott, 1832.
ixth " " " " " Scott, 1832, to the Present Time.

In the case of American writers the "Eras" are not used, as contemporaneity is of small consequence; it may be added that less exclusiveness has been thought desirable in the case of those belonging to our own country.

The classification of authors and literary forms is believed to be at once simple and exhaustive: if this belief be well-founded, there will be one less want among the many which oppress the earnest scholar.

Literary forms may be reduced to nine :

1. Letter.	2. Essay.	3. Treatise.	Written.
4. Tale.	5. Narration.	6. History.	Written or Spoken.
7. Oration.	8. Address.	9. Lecture.	Spoken.

The Letter, Tale, and Oration agree in their standpoint, which is that of the author, and in their aim, which is to impress.

The Essay, Narration, and Address recognize the standpoint of both author and reader, are tentative, and aim to stimulate.

The Treatise, History, and Lecture assume the standpoint of the reader, are exhaustive in their mode of treatment, and aim to convince.

For the classification of literary forms, the distinctions of Prose and Verse are not essential, but the reader will be able to distinguish the Prose works by the italicising of their titles.

Authors are classified by their work and not by their personal biographies. The object of any classification should be to group those whose *manner of treatment* is alike rather than those who deal variously with *similar subjects*. A humorous person, in so far as he is a humorist, will treat humorously any subject, even if it be history or metaphysics. A satirist, so long as he continues a satirist, will treat every subject satirically ; hence the character of the work will be determined by the bias of the writer, and not at all by his selection of themes. A valid classification will thus be limited by the possible *phases of the human mind.* Seven phases seem sufficient for the expression of mental differences, and while the complete man will manifest each one of them, less gifted mortals will be limited to one or to several.

1. Critic,	whose treatment of themes	is judicial.	
2. Satirist,	"	"	recognizes only contradictions.
3. Humorist,	"	"	regards simply seeming irrationalities.
4. Sentimentalist,	"	"	is based upon the feelings.
5. Rhetorician,	"	"	regards mainly effectiveness of presentation.
6. Metaphysician,	"	"	is speculative.
7. Physicist,	"	"	is based upon experiment.

He to whom each of these manifestations is but a phase, is alone the master artist, poet, philosopher, or man ; such are indeed "not one but all mankind's epitome," and these are the immortal few whose reputation and whose influence is confined to no country, and to no times.

Representative Works only have been named.

The Characterization consists of criticisms which fairly represent the strength and weakness of the author : and these criticisms have as far as possible been taken from critics whose opinion is known by all to be beyond dispute ; as soon as a critic transcends the limit assigned to him by the world at large, his opinion is not presented.

Finally, this little book is offered for its serviceableness ; if it lacks merit, the author would not care to give it any factitious aid by extended reference to authorities, or by any recital of his own possible fitness for the office which he has undertaken to fill.

H. H. M.

St. Louis, *January*, 1875.

AUTHOR.	CLASS.	FORM.	REPRESENTATIVE WORKS.
1. ADDISON, JOSEPH 1672–1719. Era VI.	Sentimentalist.	Letter. Essay. Tale. History.	Letter to Lord Halifax. Essays in The Spectator. Poems. Cato.
2. BACON, FRANCIS 1561–1626. III.	Physicist.	Essay. Treatise. History.	Essays. Instauratio Magna. History of Henry VII.
3. BROWNING, ELIZABETH B. 1809–1861. IX.	Sentimentalist.	Tale. Narration. Essay.	Portuguese Sonnets. Casa Guidi Windows. Aurora Leigh. The Greek Christian Poets.
4. BROWNING, ROBERT 1812– IX.	Metaphysician.	Narration. History.	My Last Duchess. Blot on the 'Scutcheon.
5. BUNYAN, JOHN 1628–1688. V.	Sentimentalist.	Narration.	Pilgrim's Progress.
6. BURNS, ROBERT 1759–1796. VIII.	Sentimentalist. Satirist. Humorist.	Tale. Narration.	Address to the De'il. John Anderson. Mouse. Daisy. Bannockburn. Cottar's Saturday Night. Tam O'Shanter.
7. BUTLER, SAMUEL 1612–1680. V.	Satirist.	Narration.	Hudibras.
8. BYRON, LORD 1788–1824. VIII.	Rhetorician. Satirist.	Essay. Tale. Narration. History.	English Bards and Scotch Reviewers. Prisoner of Chillon. Mazeppa. Don Juan. Childe Harold. Manfred.
9. BULWER, EDW'D LYTTON 1805–1873. IX	Rhetorician.	Narration.	Pelham. The Caxtons. My Novel.

CHARACTERIZATION.	*REMARKS.*
" To attain a style familiar but not coarse, elegant but not ostentatious, one must give his days and nights to Addison."—*Dr. Sam'l Johnson.* " A polished shaft in the temple of letters, we are more struck with the beauty of workmanship, than with the weight supported."—*Prof. John Bascom.*	Addison formed Simple Prose Style. The subjects treated in the Spectator series are mainly Fashions and Follies, although the Criticism upon Paradise Lost is the subject of several papers. Addison was a noted " conversationist."
" Comprehensiveness of mind and power of condensed thought; closest reasoning in the boldest metaphor."—*T. B. Shaw.* " Most discriminating and refined observations upon human life."—*Edmund Burke.*	Bacon's Essays have furnished the thoughts of many books; his place in science has not been settled, despite the numerous essays upon his claims.
" Style rugged and unfinished, often without rhythm. Moral purpose, deep emotion, high-toned thought and devout spirit. Rises to heights on which man has never stood, and finds depths which he has never fathomed."—*T. B. Shaw.*	Translator of Prometheus Bound.
"' The Blot on the 'Scutcheon ' is the finest poem of the century."—*Chas. Dickens.* " Constructs character from within ; a thinker rather than a singer. Style abrupt and harsh."—*British Quarterly Review,* 6—1847.	Browning's poetry is distinguished by the essential characteristics of the great masters of " Classical Music."
" Style delightful to every reader and invaluable as a study to every person who wishes to obtain a wide command over language, magnificence, pathos, vehement exhortation, subtle disquisition."—*T. B. Macaulay.*	
" Great humor, pathos, descriptive power, discrimination of character."—*Francis Jeffrey.* " Wanted everything for completeness ; culture, leisure, true effort, length of life itself. Excellence—his indisputable air of truth."—*Thomas Carlyle.*	The first distinguished Scottish poet after the separation of English and Scotch as languages.
" Still the most prominent work in the literature of satire; wit, ingenuity, style concise and suggestive. His expressions have the terse strength of proverbs and open boundless vistas of comic associations."—*Geo. S. Hillard.*	Butler's minor poems contain much for the the lovers of satire.
" Unrivalled in description and expression of passion; power over the resources of language great, although he is not a careful or accurate writer. His poetry abounds in passages of melting tenderness and exquisite sweetness, in wit playful and brilliant, in sarcasm venomous and blistering. Leading characteristic is energy; never tame, in his higher moods his words flash and burn like lightning."—*Geo. S. Hillard.*	Byron's love for inanimate nature and for liberty was genuine, and hence he reaches his " high-water mark " in these directions. Possessed by a spirit of *unbelief* and yet unable to attain *disbelief,* he lacked " themes " real to himself, falling as he did upon times of transition.
" Delineator of the passion of love."—*Bayne.* " In the highest qualities required in this branch of composition [the novel] Sir Edward Lytton Bulwer stands pre-eminent, and entitled to a place beside Scott himself, at the very head of the prose writers of works of imagination in our country."—*Sir A. Alison.*	

AUTHOR.	CLASS.	FORM.	REPRESENTATIVE WORKS.
10. CAMPBELL, THOMAS 1777–1844. VIII.	Sentimentalist.	Tale. Narration.	Hohenlinden. Ye Mariners of England. Gertrude of Wyoming.
11. CARLYLE, THOMAS 1795– IX.	Sentimentalist. Satirist.	Essay. History.	Hero and Hero-Worship. Sartor Resartus. Frederick the Great. Life and Letters of Cromwell. History of the French Revolution.
12. CHAUCER, GEOFFREY 1328–1400. I.	Humorist. Sentimentalist. Physicist.	Tale. Narration.	A Ballad teaching what is Gentleness. Chaucer's A B C. Legend of Good Women. Complaint of Venus and Mars. Canterbury Tales.
13. CHESTERFIELD, EARL OF 1694–1773. VI.	Rhetorician.	Letter.	Letters to his Son.
14. COLERIDGE, SAMUEL T. 1772–1834. IX.	Metaphysician.	Essay. Tale. Lecture.	The Friend. Ode to France. Chamouni. Lectures on Shakespeare.
15. COWLEY, ABRAHAM 1618–1667. IV.	Metaphysician.	Tale.	Davideis. Anacreontics. The Mistress.
16. COWPER, WILLIAM 1731–1800. VIII.	Sentimentalist. Humorist.	Letter. Tale. Narration.	To the Rev. John Newton. John Gilpin. Boadicea. Oaths. The Task.
17. DE FOE, DANIEL 1661–1731. V.	Physicist. Rhetorician.	Treatise. Narration. History.	Essay on Projects. Robinson Crusoe. Life of Moll Flanders. History of the Union (Scottish and English).
18. DICKENS, CHARLES 1812–1870. IX.	Rhetorician. Humorist.	Essay. Narration.	Pickwick Papers. Copperfield. Dombey and Son. Oliver Twist.

CHARACTERIZATION.	REMARKS.
"Talent for the pathetic and sublime; correctness and animation."—*Francis Jeffrey.*	Compiler of "Specimens of the British Poets"; perhaps our best anthology.
"Assumes to be the reformer and castigator of his age; a reformer in philosophy, politics, and religion, denouncing the mechanical way of thinking and want of faith, and yet has no distinct dogma, creed, or constitution to promulgate; his style is his own, and combines all possible faults."—*Blackwood's Magazine.*	Carlyle is an iconoclast and fell upon times of transition. Of the effectiveness of his work the world bears witness; of its value in exciting inquiry there can be no doubt.
"His manly cheerfulness is especially delicious to me in my old age."—*S. T. Coleridge.* "There was wanted some one not only endowed with poetic genius and an intellect cultivated with the best scholarship of the age, but also, in addition to the love of books, familiarity with the human heart gained by intercourse with men in the arena of actual life."—*E. P. Whipple.*	
"Lord Chesterfield's ideal of excellence was essentially superficial; his praise of solid acquirement and genuine principles is always coupled with the assertion of their entire inutility if unaccompanied by grace, external polish, and an agreeable manifestation. . . . Rhetoric, in his view, transcends reflective power."—*H. T. Tuckerman.*	An expurgated edition of Lord Chesterfield's Letters has been published by Dr. Trusler. Chesterfield is still the best authority on manners.
"Seeks ideal truth; predominant habit, in-looking; irregular imagination, with reflective meditation."—*Henry Reed.* "'Ode to France,' the finest in modern times."—*Shelley.* "Largest and most spacious intellect, subtlest and most comprehensive of men."—*Thomas De Quincey.*	
"Replete with learning and all the ornaments supplied by books." —*Dr. Samuel Johnson.*	Best of the "Concetti."
"Language has masculine vigor and idiomatic strength; sentiments from the heart."—*Thomas Campbell.* "Redeemed poetical language."—*Francis Jeffrey.*	Restored to poetry the use of simple language, and vindicated the claims of "the poetry of ordinary life."
"Great ingenuity, strong and clear conceptions; language equally perspicuous and forcible."—*C. D. Cleveland.*	Partisan criticism harassed De Foe during life, and after death it, to a great extent, persuaded the world that his sole claim to recollection rested upon Robinson Crusoe. Allibone states De Foe's works to be 210 in number.
"Peculiar and original vein of humor; quaint, grotesque, and unexpected combination of ideas. Excels in scenes of sickness or death, and has uncommon skill in the minute representation of scenes of still life. Tone sound and healthy, poetical imagination, hatred of injustice and oppression."—*Geo. S. Hillard.*	

AUTHOR.	CLASS.	FORM.	REPRESENTATIVE WORKS.
19. DRYDEN, JOHN 1631–1700. v.	Rhetorician. Satirist.	Letter. Essay. Treatise. Tale. Narration. History.	Epistle to Congreve. *Prefaces.* *Essay on Dramatic Poetry.* Ode to St. Cecilia. Absalom and Achitophel. The Indian Emperor.
20. ELIOT, GEORGE 1820– IX.	Metaphysician.	Tale. Narration.	Poems. *Adam Bede. Romola. Middlemarch.*
21. FIELDING, HENRY 1707–1754. VII.	Humorist. Sentimentalist. Critic.	Essay. Narration. History.	*On Conversation.* *Tom Jones. Amelia.* Dramas.
22. GIBBON, EDWARD 1737–1794. VIII.	Rhetorician.	History.	*Decline and Fall of the Roman Empire.*
23. GOLDSMITH, OLIVER 1728–1774. VII.	Humorist. Sentimentalist. Rhetorician.	Essay. Treatise. Narration. History.	*Citizen of the World.* *Animated Nature.* *Vicar of Wakefield.* Deserted Village. The Traveller. *She Stoops to Conquer.*
24. GRAY, THOMAS 1716–1771. VII.	Sentimentalist. Rhetorician.	Tale. Essay. Letter.	Elegy in a Country Churchyard. Progress of Poesy. *Letters to West, Walpole, and others.*

CHARACTERIZATION.	*REMARKS.*

"A writer of a manly and elastic character; strong judgment gives force and direction to a flexible fancy. Lacks intense or lofty sensibility; coarse, characters too abstract."—*Thomas Campbell.*

Dryden gave us the versified letter, the first specimen of prose style, and the first versified personal satire. The Ode to St. Cecilia (popularly called Alexander's Feast) is all that now represents Dryden's work to the general reader.

"Style of extraordinary beauty and power, choice English, limpid phrase, charming simplicity, felicity of expression. Sententious, fonder of reflection than of narration; narrative weak and commonplace; constructive and inventive faculty lacking; weak in plot, but strong in dialogue. Psychological analysis her strength and joy." —*W. C. Wilkinson.*

Marion C. Evans (Mrs. G. H. Lewes). Perhaps the best review of George Eliot yet written is that of W. C. Wilkinson in Scribner's, Oct., 1874; the strictures of "The Nation" may be read as a corrective for any over-statement.

"The prose Homer of human nature."—*Lord Byron.*
"The romance of 'Tom Jones,' that exquisite picture of human manners, will outlive the palace of the Escurial and the imperial eagle of Austria."—*Gibbon.*
"Fielding will ever remain the delight of his country, and will always retain his place in the libraries of Europe, notwithstanding the unfortunate grossness,—the mark of an uncultivated taste." . . . . —*Sir James Mackintosh.*

"Gibbon was not, like Hume, a self-thinking, deep-fathoming man, who searched into the nature of things, existence, and thought, ... but had the capacity of quickly making other people's thoughts and investigations his own, and of propounding them in an admirable manner."—*Schlosser.*
"But the whole is, notwithstanding, such an assemblage of merits, so various, so interesting, so rare, that the History of the Decline and Fall must always be considered as one of the most extraordinary monuments that have appeared of the literary powers of a single mind, and its fame can perish only with the civilization of the world."—*Prof. Smyth.*

Gibbon is oftenest and most justly reproached with his infidelity; and it is after granting the justice of the complaints on the part of the Christian, the moralist, the historian, and the man of taste, that Professor Smyth makes his statement. Allibone's article upon Gibbon will guide more extended inquiry.

"Wrote to exalt virtue and to expose vice."—*Walter Scott.*
"Purity of moral lesson, and interest of story."—*C. D. Cleveland.*
"The delineations of this character [that of the "excellent Wakefield"] on his course of life through joys and sorrows, the ever-increasing interest of the story, ... make this novel one of the best that was ever written."—*Goethe.*
"Goldsmith, both in verse and prose, was one of the most delightful writers in the language. His verse flows like a limpid stream." —*William Hazlitt.*

"Energy, splendor, and perfect finish of poetical style."—*George S. Hillard.*

Founded the school of "reflective poetry, occupying itself with the feelings and interests of ordinary life."

AUTHOR.	CLASS.	FORM.	REPRESENTATIVE WORKS.
25. GROTE, GEORGE 1794–1871. IX.	Rhetorician.	History.	*History of Greece.*

26. HALLAM, HENRY 1778–1859. VIII.	Critic.	History.	*View of Europe during the Middle Ages.* *The Constitutional History of England.* *Introduction to the Literature of Europe* *in the 15th, 16th, and 17th Centuries.*
27. HAZLITT, WILLIAM 1778–1830. VIII.	Rhetorician. Sentimentalist.	Essay. History. Lecture.	*Characters of Shakespeare's Plays. Es-* *says on English Novelists.* *Life of Napoleon.* *Lectures on Authors.*
28. HEMANS, FELICIA D. 1793–1835. VIII.	Sentimentalist.	Tale. Narration.	Bernardo del Carpio. *Tales and Historic Scenes.*
29. HERBERT, GEORGE 1593–1632. III.	Sentimentalist.	Tale.	The Temple.
30. HOOD, THOMAS 1798–1845. IX.	Humorist. Sentimentalist.	Tale. Narration.	Song of the Shirt. Lady's Dream. *Whims and Oddities.* Bridge of Sighs. *Tylney Hall.*
31. HUME, DAVID 1711–1776. VIII.	Metaphysician.	Essay. History.	*Essays, Moral and Metaphysical.* *History of England.*

CHARACTERIZATION.

"A decided liberal, perhaps even a republican, in politics, Mr. Grote has labored to counteract the influence of Mr. Mitford in Grecian history, and to construct a history of Greece from authentic materials, which should illustrate the animating influence of democratic freedom upon the exertions of the human mind. . . . . He has displayed an extent of learning, a variety of research, a power of combination, which are worthy of the very highest praise, and which have secured for him a lasting place among the historians of modern times."—*Sir A. Alison.*

"Spirit of fairness and impartiality; style dry, austere, uniformly clear; sometimes overloaded with ornament."—*T. B. Macaulay.*

"All the subjects glanced at in these earlier lectures [his own] are there [H.'s Middle Ages] thoroughly considered by this author with all the patience of an antiquarian, and the spirit and sagacity of a philosopher."—*Prof. Smyth.*

"In extent and variety of learning, and a deep acquaintance with antiquarian lore, the historian of the Middle Ages may deservedly take a place with the most eminent writers in that style that Europe has produced."—*Sir A. Alison.*

"When Mr. Hazlitt's taste and judgment are left to themselves, we think him among the best, if not the very best, of living critics in our national literature; . . . . he is sometimes the very worst. One would suppose that he had a personal quarrel with all living writers, good, bad, and indifferent. . . . . With him, to be alive is not only a fault, but it includes all other possible faults. . . . In short, if you want his praise, you must die for it; and when such praise is deserved, and given *con amore*, it is almost worth dying for."—*Christopher North.*

"Infinitely sweet, tender, and elegant; contemplative rather than vehement; exquisite delicacy, evenness of execution, purity and loftiness of feeling; humble tone of indulgence and piety, diction beautifully harmonious and free."—*Francis Jeffrey.*

"Next to the Scripture poems, there are none so savory to me as Mr. George Herbert's."—*Richard Baxter.*

"Accurate observer of life and manners; wit arises from a profusion of quaint, odd, and unexpected combinations; humor rich and delicate; without rival as a punster."—*George S. Hillard.*

"Negligent in the use of the sources of history."—*Schlosser.*

"As an elegant and spirited composition it merits every commendation. Hume always inclines to prerogative."—*Prof. Smyth.*

REMARKS.

Hallam gave us our first reliable history of literature.

Mrs. Hemans is especially the poet of the "domestic affections."

Among the few authors of good religious lyrics.

First of English humorists in order of time as well as in point of merit. His pathetic pieces are the first poetical treatment of the poor and destitute, when such treatment is used as an instrument of reform.

"His aim is to establish a universal skepticism, and to produce in the reader a complete distrust in his own faculties. . . . With the single exception of Bayle, he has carried this skeptical mode of reasoning farther than any modern philosopher."—*Dug. Stewart.*

AUTHOR.	*CLASS.*	*FORM.*	*REPRESENTATIVE WORKS.*
32. JEFFREY, FRANCIS 1773–1850. VIII.	Critic.	Essay.	*Contributions to Edinburgh Review.*
33. JERROLD, DOUGLAS 1803–1857. IX	Humorist.	Essay. History.	*Caudle Lectures. Heads of the People.* Black-Eyed Susan. Rent-Day.
34. JOHNSON, SAMUEL 1709–1784. VII.	Sentimentalist.	Tale. Essay. Treatise. Narration. History.	*Rasselas.* *The Rambler.* *Lives of the Poets.* London. Irene.
35. JONSON, BEN 1573–1637. III.	Rhetorician. Humorist.	Tale. History.	Epigrams. Epitaph for Shakespeare. Volpone. Catiline. The Alchemist. *Every Man in his Humor.* Sejanus.
36. JUNIUS 1769–1772. VII.	Satirist.	Letter.	*The Letters of Junius.*
37. KEATS, JOHN 1796–1820. VIII.	Rhetorican.	Tale.	Endymion. Hyperion. Lamia. Isa- bella. Eve of St. Agnes. Hymn to Pan. Ode to a Nightingale.
38. LAMB, CHARLES 1775–1834. VIII.	Humorist. Sentimentalist.	Letter. Essay. Tale. Narration. History.	*Letter to a Distant Correspondent.* *Essays of Elia.* Poetry for Children. *Tales from the Plays of Shakespeare.* John Woodvil.

CHARACTERIZATION.

" Thoroughly acquainted with progress and pretensions of modern literature and philosophy; the natural acuteness and discrimination of the logician, with habitual caution and coolness. . . . . His strength consists in a great range of knowledge, an equal familiarity with the principles and with the details of a subject, and in a glancing brilliancy and rapidity of style."—*William Hazlitt.*

" Rare skill, undoubted originality, imperturbable good temper, . . . a flash of wit at once dazzling and delightful."—*London Athenæum.*

" Pomp and uniformity."—*William Hazlitt.*

" Style artificial, elaborate, delighting in antithesis and words of Latin origin; frequently pompous and heavy."—*George S. Hillard.*

Dr. Johnson, as a man and as a moral influence, is still one of the great names in human history; as a writer, his works have been replaced by others better adapted to the wants of our own time. He was also a noted conversationist, gave us an edition of Shakespeare, and the first English dictionary.

" Jonson possessed all the learning that was wanting to Shakespeare, and wanted all the genius which the other possessed."—*David Hume.*

" His works, as the characteristic productions of an individual mind, or as records of the manners of a particular age, cannot be valued too highly; but they have little charm for the more general reader."—*William Hazlitt.*

" Classic purity of language, extensive information, force and perspicuity of argument, fearless and decisive tone, severity of reproach, attachment to the principles of the constitution."—*J. M. Good.*

The authorship of these letters is still unsettled. For a full discussion of this subject see Allibone's Dictionary of Authors.

" Power of language, rays of fancy, gleams of genius; unintelligible, rugged, diffuse, tiresome, absurd."—*Gifford.*

" Wonderful profusion of figurative language, often exquisitely beautiful and luxuriant, but sometimes fantastical and far-fetched. Strain of classic imagery, combined with a perception of natural loveliness rich and delicate."—*T. B. Shaw.*

Keats began the " scholarly school of poetry "; a school which seeks its themes in the glories of the past and which, while in the present, is not of the present.

" A true poet, but not a great one."—*D. M. Moir.*

" Fine humor, taste, penetration, vivacity, delicacy of feeling, and happiness of expression. Style marked by quaintness and antiqueness."—*T. B. Shaw.*

" I know of no essay-writing comparable to them [the Essays of Elia], so full are they of an inimitable blending of thoughtfulness and playfulness,—that half-serious, half-sportive habit of mind, far more agreeable than wit, described by our word . . . . humor."—*Henry Reed.*

Gave us specimens of the English dramatic poets.

2

AUTHOR.	CLASS.	FORM.	REPRESENTATIVE WORKS.
39. LOCKE, JOHN 1632–1704. V.	Metaphysician.	Treatise.	Essay on the Limits of the Human Under- standing. Treatise on Government. Thoughts concerning the Education of Children.
40. LOCKHART, J. G. 1794–1854. IX.	Rhetorician.	Essay. Narration. History.	Peter's Letters to his Kinsfolk. Contri- butions to London Quarterly. Valerius; a Roman Story. Adam Blair. Reginald Dalton. History of the Late War. Life of Burns. Life of Napoleon. Life of Scott.
41. MACAULAY, T. B. 1800–1859. IX.	Rhetorician.	Essay. Tale. History.	Essays. Lays of Ancient Rome. History of England.
42. MARLOWE, CHRISTOPHER 1563–1593. III.	Rhetorician.	Tale. History.	Passionate Shepherd to his Love. Tamburlane the Great. Edward II. Dr. Faustus. The Jew of Malta.
43. MASSINGER, PHILIP 1584–1640. III.	Rhetorician.	History.	Duke of Milan. The Virgin Martyr. The Unnatural Combat.
44. MILTON, JOHN 1608–1674. IV.	Rhetorician. Sentimentalist.	Essay. Treatise. Tale. Narration. History.	Controversial Tracts. On Divorce. On the Morning of Christ's Nativity. Lycidas. Paradise Lost. Paradise Regained. Comus. Samson Agonistes.
45. MONTGOMERY, JAMES 1771–1854. VIII.	Sentimentalist.	Tale. Narration. Treatise.	Hymns. Pelican Island. Lectures on Poetry and General Literature.
46. MOORE, TOM 1779–1852. VIII.	Sentimentalist. Humorist.	Tale. Narration.	Irish Melodies. National Melodies. Lalla Rookh. Fudge Family in Paris.
47. MORE, HANNAH 1745–1833. VIII.	Sentimentalist.	Tale. Essay. Narration. History.	Tales in Verse. On Female Education. Thoughts on the Manners of the Great. Cœlebs in Search of a Wife. Percy. The Inflexible Captive.

CHARACTERIZATION.   *REMARKS.*

"In language of all philosophers the most figurative, ambiguous, various, vacillating, and even contradictory."—*Reid.*

"Solicitous only to convey his ideas with perspicuity and precision, no affectations, no conceits, no daring metaphors, no inverted sentences: clear, easy, natural."—*Drake.*

"In the lighter branches of literature he has deservedly attained the very highest eminence. As a moralist, a critic, and a biographer, he has taken a leading place in English literature."—*Sir A. Alison.*

Fine translations of ancient Spanish ballads.

"Brilliant rhetorical power, splendid coloring, affluence of illustration, animation, and energy."—*George S. Hillard.*

"It is this partial and one-sided exposition of the truth, accompanied by a generally exaggerated style of composition, more than positive inaccuracy, that we complain of in Mr. Macaulay."—*Sir A. Alison.*

"Fancy rich; feeling, tender; there is no such sweetness of versification and imagery to be found in our blank verse anterior to Shakespeare."—*Thomas Campbell.*

"The reluctant pangs of abdicating royalty in Edward furnished hints which Shakespeare scarcely improved in his Richard II.; and the death-scene of Marlowe's King moves pity and terror beyond any scene, ancient or modern, with which I am acquainted."—*Chas. Lamb.*

Marlowe's is the second great name in dramatic literature.

"Certainly the best historical plays after Shakespeare's."—*Henry Hallam.*

"Wit, sprightly dialogue, theatrical effect; beauty of language, harmonious swell of numbers, pure and genuine idiom."—*Henry Hallam.*

Ranks high among the Elizabethan dramatists.

"Classical judgment and regular perfection. The subject of Paradise Lost is the finest that has ever been chosen for heroic poetry; it is also managed by Milton with admirable skill."—*Henry Hallam.*

"The only blank verse except Shakespeare's."—*William Hazlitt.*

"Purity of feeling, and gentle, sympathetic spirit; many noble descriptions, but lacks strength for protracted flight; genius essentially lyric."—*George S. Hillard.*

"Vivid fancy, sparkling wit, rich command of poetical expression, love of ornament, sense of music; not careful, and will not bear verbal criticism."—*George S. Hillard.*

"She did, perhaps, as much real good in her generation as any woman that ever held the pen. Style flowing and sparkling with a pleasant humor."—*T. B. Shaw.*

	AUTHOR.	CLASS.	FORM.	REPRESENTATIVE WORKS.
48.	POPE, ALEXANDER 1688-1744. VI.	Rhetorician. Satirist.	Letter. Essay. Tale. Narration. Treatise.	Eloise to Abelard. Epistles. Preface to Edition of Shakespeare. Rape of the Lock. The Dunciad. On Criticism. On Man.
49.	QUINCEY, THOMAS DE 1785-1859. IX.	Rhetorician.	Essay. Treatise. Narration. History	Miscellaneous Essays. English Poets and Writers. The Logic of Political Economy. The Cæsars. Confessions of an Opium-Eater. Bio- graphical Sketches.
50.	ROBERTSON, WILLIAM 1721-1793. VIII.	Rhetorician.	History.	Histories of America, Scotland, and of Charles V.
51.	ROGERS, SAMUEL 1763-1855. VIII.	Rhetorician.	Tale. Narration.	Ginevra. Pleasures of Memory. Columbus. Italy.
52.	RUSKIN, JOHN 1819– IX.	Rhetorician. Sentimentalist.	Essay. Lecture.	Stones of Venice. Giotto and his Works in Padua. Modern Painters. Seven Lamps of Architecture. Lectures on Architecture and Painting.
53.	RUSSELL, WILLIAM H. 1816– IX.	Rhetorician.	Letter.	Correspondence for London Times.
54.	SCOTT, SIR WALTER 1771-1832. VIII.	Sentimentalist.	Tale. Narration. History.	Songs. Marmion. Waverley. Ivanhoe. Ken- ilworth. Lady of the Lake. Lay of the Last Minstrel.- Lives of Dryden, Swift, Napoleon.

CHARACTERIZATION.	*REMARKS.*

"Compact and pointed diction."—*Macaulay.*

"Strictest melody and tersest expression; pauses have too little variety, phrases too antithetical."—*Thomas Campbell.*

"Rhymes defective; uniformly smooth and melodious."—*William Hazlitt.*

"Reasoning without imagination or sentiment."—*Sir E. Brydges.*

"Condensation of thought."—*Shenstone.*

REMARKS.

Almost all of Pope's literary forms became new under his management. His translation of Homer, while not valuable as a translation, is nevertheless one of the most beautiful of English poems.

"Graphic power, accuracy of detail with poetic illustration."—*London Monthly Review.*

"Pungency, brevity, force."—*M'Culloch.*

"Acute perception of character, classic elegance of style; lacks narrative power, but has power of picturesque description."—*W. H. Prescott.*

"Master of English composition, critic of uncommon delicacy, unflinching investigator of received opinions, philosophic inquirer second only to Coleridge."—*London Quarterly Review.*

"Uses spoken English."—*Burke.*

"Good sense and elegance."—*Mackintosh.*

"Robertson is your Livy; his Charles V. is written with truth."—*Voltaire.*

"Careful finish and the grace of patient elaboration."—*George S. Hillard.*

"Lacks logical faculty; style perspicuous and forcible when not inflated."—*Edinburgh Review.*

"Unstable, crotchety, passionate, too intense at times to be just, still they [his works] contain worlds of thought, imagination, and knowledge, such as no other artist can educe. A strong and earnest purpose runs through them all, given to the highest ends."—*London Athenæum.*

Gives us an account of the Crimean War.

"Genuine human worth."—*Thomas Carlyle.*

"Secret of popularity and leading characteristic,—common topics, images, and expressions. Aptitude for description of scenes abounding in motion or action of any kind."—*Francis Jeffrey.*

"Most intensely real representation of the living spirit of the chivalrous age. His poetry might make a very coward fearless."—*Christopher North.*

"Men fashioned of human earth and warm with human sympathies."—*T. N. Talfourd.*

"Versification easy and graceful, thought sometimes careless; style energetic and condensed; pictures glowing and faithful; characters and incidents fresh and startling; battle-scenes rival the pages of Homer."—*George S. Hillard.*

AUTHOR.	CLASS.	FORM.	REPRESENTATIVE WORKS.
55. SHAKESPEARE, WILLIAM 1564–1616. III.	Sentimentalist. Rhetorician. Critic. Humorist. Satirist. Metaphysician. Physicist.	Tale. History.	Sonnets. Hamlet. The Tempest. Julius Cæsar. Macbeth. Lear. Merchant of Venice. Merry Wives of Windsor.
56. SHELLEY, PERCY BYSSHE 1792–1822. VIII.	Sentimentalist. Metaphysician.	Tale. Narration. History.	The Skylark. Adonais. The Sensitive Plant. Queen Mab. Alastor. Prometheus Unbound. The Cenci.
57. SHERIDAN, R. B. 1751–1816. VIII.	Humorist. Sentimentalist.	History. Oration.	The Rivals. School for Scandal. The Critic. Speech in the Trial of Hastings.
58. SMITH, SYDNEY 1771–1845. VIII.	Humorist.	Letter. Essay.	Letters on the Subject of the Catholics, to my Brother Abraham who lives in the Country. Contributions to the Edinburgh Review.
59. SOUTHEY, ROBERT 1774–1843. IX.	Rhetorician.	Letter. Essay. Tale. Narration. History.	Letters written from Spain and Portugal. Articles from Magazines and Reviews. Well of St. Keyne. Mary, the Maid of the Inn. A Tale of Paraguay. Madoc. Joan of Arc. Thalaba the Destroyer. Biographies. History of Brazil. History of the Peninsular War.
60. SPENSER, EDMUND 1553–1599. III.	Rhetorician.	Tale. Narration. Treatise.	Mother Hubbard's Tale. The Faery Queen. Astrophel. View of the State of Ireland.
61. STERNE, LAURENCE 1713–1769. VII.	Satirist. Rhetorician.	Narration.	Tristram Shandy.

CHARACTERIZATION.

Shakespeare being confessedly the first name in literature, all characterizations take the form of eulogiums. Perhaps the best thing that has been said (not to except Coleridge's epithet) is that "Shakespeare possessed a capacity for universal knowledge without universal experience."—*W. C. Wilkinson.*

"Some of the metaphysical and ethical theories of Shelley were certainly most absurd and pernicious. No modern poet has possessed in equal degree the highest qualities of the great ancient masters."—*Macaulay.*

"Dramatic star of the first magnitude."—*William Hazlitt.*

"He is universally admitted to have been a great reasoner, and the greatest master of ridicule that has appeared among us since Swift."—*Macaulay.*

"Of all his chief poems the conception and execution are original: in much faulty, and imperfect in both; but bearing throughout the impress of original power, and breathing a moral charm in the midst of the wildest and sometimes even extravagant imaginings."—*Christopher North.*

"Mr. Southey's prose style can scarcely be too much praised. It is plain, clear, pointed, familiar, perfectly modern in its texture, but with a grave and sparkling admixture of archaisms in its ornaments."—*William Hazlitt.*

"We must not fear to assert, with the best judges of this and of former ages, that Spenser is still the third name in the poetical literature of our country, and that he has not been surpassed, except by Dante, in any other."—*Henry Hallam.*

"His command of imagery is wide, easy, and luxuriant. He threw the soul of harmony into our verse, and made it more warmly, tenderly, and magnificently descriptive than it ever was before, or, with few exceptions, than it has ever been since. It must certainly be owned that in description he exhibits nothing of the brief strokes and robust power which characterize the very greatest poets."—*Thomas Campbell.*

"Indecency and affectation. . . . . In power of touching the finer feelings of the heart, he has never been excelled."—*Voltaire.*

"The pure essence of English conversational style."—*William Hazlitt.*

REMARKS.

Allibone gives a full list of Shakespearean works; and since he makes so strong a statement in regard to "The Authorship of Shakespeare," it seems not amiss to call special attention to the work of Judge Holmes. To those asking what and how much was Shakespeare, the best answer will be given by the Lectures of Coleridge, and by a series of articles in "The Journal of Speculative Philosophy."

"These (Plymley Letters) perhaps did as much towards promoting Catholic Emancipation as all other publications and speeches together."—*S. Austen Allibone.*

To the poet, Spenser addresses himself by his versification and fancy, and hence he has impressed himself upon all the excellent poets since his time. To the lover of Froissart, Spenser will always be dear. "Fluidity" of language and verse, fancy, harmony, imagery, cleanliness, and purity,—these qualities are undeniably his; but his works, to the general reader, are but "the bricks and mortar" of a noble structure.

AUTHOR.	CLASS.	FORM.	REPRESENTATIVE WORKS.
62. SWIFT, JONATHAN 1667–1745. VI.	Satirist. Humorist.	Letter. Essay. Treatise. Tale. Narration.	*Correspondence.* *Political Pamphlets.* *Drapier Letters.* *Tale of a Tub.* Poems to Stella. *Gulliver's Travels.*
63. TALFOURD, T. N. 1795–1854. IX.	Rhetorician.	Essay. Narration. History.	*Critical and Miscellaneous Essays.* Poems. Ion : a Tragedy.
64. TENNYSON, ALFRED 1810– IX.	Sentimentalist. Rhetorician.	Tale. Narration.	Lady Clara Vere de Vere. Maud. In Memoriam. The Princess. Idyls of the King.
65. THACKERAY, W. M. 1811–1863. IX.	Satirist. Humorist.	Essay. Tale. Narration.	*Addison. Steele. Goldsmith.* End of the Play. *Vanity Fair. Pendennis. The New-comes.*
66. THOMSON, JAMES 1700–1748. VII.	Sentimentalist.	Narration.	The Seasons. Castle of Indolence.
67. WALLER, EDMUND 1605–1687. IV.	Sentimentalist.	Tale.	Go, lovely Rose.
68. WATTS, ISAAC 1674–1748. VI.	Sentimentalist.	Tale. Treatise.	Hymns. *Improvement of the Mind.*

CHARACTERIZATION.	*REMARKS.*

"In humor and irony, in the talent of debasing and defiling what he hated, we join with the world in thinking the Dean of St. Patrick's without rival."—*Francis Jeffrey.*

"His style is, in its kind, one of the models of English composition; it is proper, pure, precise, perspicuous, significant, nervous, deriving a certain dignity from a masterly contempt of puerile ornaments." —*Mackintosh.*

"Many of Talfourd's critical essays are remarkable for refinement of observation and frequent felicity of phrase, [but] there is hardly one of them which is brought to a close without being partially impaired by that flux of words which was his bane."—*North British Review.*

Talfourd's essays are classed with those of the "Modern British Essayists."

"There is no finer ear, nor more command of language, but he wants a subject."—*R. W. Emerson.*

"'In Memoriam' comes more intimately home to English sympathies than Lycidas or Adonais, and may be pointed to, perhaps, as the one special monody to which beauty of form and feeling have given a universal currency."—*London Athenæum.*

"Versification broken and irregular, but inexpressibly charming; sometimes fantastic. Of the living poets of England, Tennyson at this time occupies the highest rank."—*Sir A. Alison.*

"Power—sustained perfection of style."—*Edinburgh Review.*

"One of the greatest of novelists; model of style and criticism."— *T. B. Shaw.*

"It is Thackeray's aim to represent life as it is actually and historically,—men and women as they are, in those situations in which they are usually placed, with that mixture of good and evil, and of strength and foible, which is to be found in their characters, and liable only to those incidents which are of ordinary occurrence."—*David Masson.*

"Every stanza of that charming allegory [Castle of Indolence], at least the whole of the first part of it, gives out a group of images from which the mind is reluctant to part, and a flow of harmony which the ear wishes to hear repeated."—*Thomas Campbell.*

"Thomson is the best of our descriptive poets."—*William Hazlitt.*

"First to paint the rolling mystery of the year, and to show that all its seasons were but the varied God."—*Christopher North.*

"Uniform elegance, felicity, and happiness of expression, and exemption from glaring faults."—*Henry Hallam.*

One of the best representatives of the poetry of the time of Charles II.

"Every Sabbath, in every region of the earth where his native tongue is spoken, thousands and tens of thousands of voices are sending the sacrifices of prayer and praise to God in the strains which he prepared for them a century ago."—*James Montgomery.*

AUTHOR.	CLASS.	FORM.	REPRESENTATIVE WORKS.
69. WILSON, JOHN 1785–1854. IX.	Sentimentalist.	Essay. Narration.	*Contributions to Blackwood's.* Isle of Palms. *Lights and Shadows of Scottish Life.*
70. WOLFE, CHARLES 1791–1823. VIII.	Sentimentalist.	Tale.	Burial of Sir John Moore.
71. WORDSWORTH, WILLIAM 1770–1850. IX.	Metaphysician.	Tale. Narration.	Ode on Immortality. Skylark. Liberty. London Early Morning. The Excursion. Tintern Abbey.
72. YOUNG, EDWARD 1681–1765. VII.	Sentimentalist.	Narration.	Night Thoughts.

CHARACTERIZATION.

" Ardent and enthusiastic genius whose eloquence is as the rush of mighty waters."—*Henry Hallam.*

" The whole literature of England does not contain a more brilliant series of articles than those with which he has enriched the pages of Blackwood's Magazine; and what is rarer still, the generosity of feeling by which they are distinguished equals their critical acuteness and delicacy of taste."—*Sir A. Alison.*

"In the lottery of literature.... Charles Wolfe has been one of the few who have drawn the prize of probable immortality from a casual gleam of inspiration thrown over a single poem.... But the lyric is indeed full of fervor and freshness, and his triumph is not to be grudged."—*D. M. Moir.*

"An austere purity of language, both grammatically and logically; in short, a perfect appropriateness of the words to the meaning. Secondly, a correspondent weight and sanity of thought and sentiment, won, not from books, but from the poet's own meditations. They are fresh and have the dew upon them..... Thirdly, the sinewy strength and originality of single lines and paragraphs; the frequent *curiosa felicitas* of his diction. Fourthly, the perfect truth of nature in his images and descriptions.... Fifthly, a meditative pathos, a union of deep and subtle thought with sensibility; a sympathy with man as man,—the sympathy, indeed, of a contemplator rather than of a fellow-sufferer and co-mate, ... but of a contemplator from whose view no difference of rank conceals the sameness of the nature. .... Lastly and pre-eminently, I challenge for this poet the gift of imagination, in the highest and strictest sense of the word."—*S. T. Coleridge.*

" Many splendid and happy conceptions, marred by false wit and overlabored antithesis: remarkably defective in progressive interest and collective effect."—*Thomas Campbell.*

" Incapable of tenderness or passion."—*Francis Jeffrey.*

John Wilson is better known as Christopher North.

An acquaintance with Wordsworth should be begun through his minor poems, e. g. To a Butterfly, Daisy, Skylark, Liberty, Immortality, Milton, Humanity, London Early Morning. His faults lie on the surface, and he has been eulogized by Talfourd, North, Southey, Hazlitt, De Quincey, Sir A. Alison, and Macaulay. A good article upon his characteristics can be found in Littell's Living Age, 1861, p. 323, or in the Fortnightly Review.

AUTHOR.	WORKS.	REASON FOR MENTION.
1. ALISON, SIR ARCHIBALD 1792-1867. IX.	History of Europe.	Leading historian and critic.
2. BEAUMONT AND FLETCHER 1586-1615. 1576-1625. III.	The Maid's Tragedy	Representative dramatists.
3. BERKELEY, BISHOP GEO. 1684-1754. VI.	Theory of Vision.	Distinguished English metaphysician.
4. BOLINGBROKE, LORD 1678-1751. VI.	Reflections on Exile. Letter to Sir William Windham.	Furnished Pope with philosophy.
5. BOSWELL, JAMES 1740-1795. VII.	Life of Johnson.	"First among biographers."—Macaulay.
6. BROUGHAM, LORD 1779-1868. IX.	Lives of Men of Letters; Reign of George III.	Distinguished as orator and statesman.
7. BROWNE, SIR THOMAS 1605-1682. IV.	Religio Medici.	Founded the grandiloquent style.
8. BUCKLE, H. T. 1823-1862. IX.	History of Civilization in England.	Leading English philosopher of civilization.
9. BURKE, EDMUND 1731-1797. VIII.	Vindication of Natural Society. Reflections on French Revolution. Letter to a Noble Lord.	England's greatest orator, and one of her most remarkable minds.
10. CHATTERTON, THOMAS 1752-1770. VII.	Tragedy of Ella. Battle of Hastings.	Known as the "Marvellous boy," and as a literary forger. "No English poet has ever equalled him at the same age."—Campbell.
11. CLARENDON, EARL OF 1608-1674. IV.	History of the Rebellion.	First contemporaneous history.
12. CROLY, GEORGE 1780-1860. VIII.	Catiline. Salathiel.	Favorite delineator of Roman thought and action.
13. CONGREVE, WILLIAM 1670-1729. V	The Old Bachelor.	Representative dramatist of the time of Charles II.

AUTHOR.	WORKS.	REASON FOR MENTION.
14. DONNE, JOHN 1573–1631. III.	Valediction Forbidding Mourning.	First of the " Concetti."
15. EVELYN, JOHN 1620–1706. IV.	Diary (1641-1706). *Terra. Sylva.*	Diary supplies the materials for a portion of history.
16. FORD, JOHN 1586–1639. III.	The Broken Heart.	Elizabethan dramatist.
17. FROUDE, JAMES A. 1818– IX.	*Short Essays on Great Subjects. History of England. History of Ireland.*	Well-known modern historian.
18. GARRICK, DAVID 1716–1779. VII.	The Lying Valet.	Restored Shakespeare to the stage.
19. HALL, J. BISHOP 1574–1656. III.	*Occasional Meditations.*	First reflective essay.
20. HERRICK, ROBERT 1591–1674. III.	Hesperides.	"Best writer of the poetry of kisses." —*Henry Hallam.*
21. HEYWOOD, THOS. –1565. II.	The English Traveller.	First known writer of Interludes.
22. HOBBES, THOMAS 1588–1679. III.	*Leviathan. Behemoth.*	First English metaphysician.
23. HOOKER, RICHARD 1553–1600. III.	*Laws of Ecclesiastical Polity.*	First figurative prose.
24. HOWELL, JAMES 1596–1666. III.	*Familiar Letters.*	First letter.
25. LINGARD, JOHN 1771–1851. VIII.	*History of England.*	Leading Catholic historian.
26. MACKINTOSH, SIR JAMES 1765–1832. VIII.	*Vindiciæ Galliæ. Contributions to Edinburgh Review. Ethical Philosophy.*	One of the British Essayists. "Great labor, ingenuity, brilliancy, and vigor; too antithetical and dogmatic." —*William Hazlitt.*

AUTHOR.	WORKS.	REASON FOR MENTION.
27. MANDEVILLE, JOHN DE 1300–1372. I.	*Travels.*	First prose. First book of travels, 1356.
28. MONTAGU, LADY MARY W. 1690–1762. VI.	*Letters.*	" Style flowing and flexible ; want of delicacy, refinement of feeling, and pure moral sentiments. Models of epistolary style."—*C. D. Cleveland.*
29. MORE, SIR THOMAS 1480–1535. II.	*Utopia. Life of Edward V.*	First history.
30. NEWTON, SIR ISAAC 1642–1727. VI.	*Philosophiæ Naturalis Principia Mathematica.*	England's first great physicist.
31. OTWAY, THOMAS 1651–1685. V.	, Venice Preserved.	Play still on the stage.
32. PEPYS, SAMUEL 1633–1703. IV.	*Pepys' Diary.*	First literary gossip.
33. PERCY, BISHOP 1728–1811. VII.	Reliques of English Poetry.	First collector of ballads.
34. READE, CHARLES 1814– IX.	*Peg Woffington. Dora.*	Leading " dramatizer."
35. RICHARDSON, SAMUEL 1689–1761. VII.	*Pamela. Clarissa Harlowe.*	First novelist, 1740.
36. RUSSELL, LADY 1636–1723. V.	*Letters.*	First literary correspondence.
37. SACKVILLE, EARL OF 1536–1608. II.	Gorboduc.	First tragedy, 1561.
38. SIDNEY, SIR PHILIP 1554–1586. III.	*Defence of Poesie.* Countess of Pembroke's Arcadia.	First literary criticism.
39. SHIRLEY, JAMES 1596–1666. III.	The Maid's Revenge.	" The last of a great race."—*Charles Lamb.*

AUTHOR.	WORKS.	REASON FOR MENTION.
40. SOUTHWELL, ROBERT 1560–1595. III.	St. Peter's Complaint.	Founder of modern religious poetry.
41. STEELE, SIR RICHARD 1675–1729. VI.	The Conscious Lovers. Christian Hero.	Began the Spectator series.
42. SURREY, EARL OF 1516–1547. II.	Translation of 2d and 4th Books of Virgil's Æneid.	First blank verse and first sonnet.
43. TEMPLE, SIR WILLIAM 1628–1698. V.	*Essay on Ancient and Modern Learning.*	With Dryden formed prose style
44. TURNER, SHARON 1768–1847. VIII.	*History of England.*	"Replete with Anglo-Saxon and other learning."—*Chancellor Kent.*
45. UDALL, NICHOLAS 1506–1557. II.	Ralph Royster Doyster.	First comedy, 1551.
46. WALPOLE, HORACE 1717–1797. VII.	*Castle of Otranto.*	First prose romance.
47. WYCHERLEY, WILLIAM 1640–1715. V.	The Way of the World.	Represents the "profligate drama."
48. WYCKLIFFE, JOHN DE 1324–1384. I.	*Translation of the Bible.*	First English Bible, 1381.

AUTHOR.	CLASS.	FORM.	REPRESENTATIVE WORKS.
1. BANCROFT, GEORGE 1800–	Critic.	History. Tale. Essay.	History of the United States. Poems. Contributions to the N. Am. Review.
2. BROWN, CHAS. BROCKDEN 1771–1810.	Rhetorician.	Narration.	Edgar Huntley.
3. BRYANT, WILLIAM CULLEN 1794–	Rhetorician.	Tale. Narration.	Thanatopsis. The Embargo. The Ages.
4. BUTLER, WILLIAM ALLEN 1825–	Satirist.	Essay. Narration.	Contributions to Democratic Review. Nothing to Wear. Two Millions.
5. CAREY, ALICE 1820–1871.	Sentimentalist.	Tale. Narration.	Poems. Clovernook. Hagar : a Story of To- day.
6. CHANNING, WM. ELLERY 1780–1842.	Metaphysician.	Essay. Address.	Milton. Napoleon. National Literature.
7. CHILD, LYDIA M. 1802–	Sentimentalist.	History. Narration.	Biographies of Good Women. Hobomok. Philothea.
8. COOPER, JAMES FENIMORE 1789–1851.	Rhetorician.	Narration. History.	Deerslayer. Red Skins. Spy. Last of the Mohecans. History of the Navy of the U. S. Lives of American Naval Officers.
9. CURTIS, GEORGE W. 1824–	Rhetorician. Humorist.	Essay. Narration. Oration.	Potiphar Papers. Nile Notes of a Howadji. Howadji in Syria. Lotos-Eaters. Duty of the American Scholar to Poli- tics and the Times.
10. EDWARDS, JONATHAN 1703–1758.	Metaphysician.	Treatise.	The Freedom of the Will and Moral Agency.
11. EMERSON, RALPH WALDO 1803–	Metaphysician.	Tale. Essay.	Poems. Conduct of Life. Representative Men.

CHARACTERIZATION.   REMARKS.

" Conscientious reference to authorities, and careful criticism."—
Heeren.
" Liberality, fairness, and research."—*Edinburgh Review.*

" He disregards rules, and cares little for criticism. But his style
is clear and nervous, ... free from affectations, indicating a singular sincerity and depth of feeling."—*R. W. Griswold.*

" In the beautiful the genius of Bryant finds its prime delight."—   Translator of Homer. Compiler of " Library
Christopher North.   of Poetry and Song." Editor N. Y. Even-
" Pure high sentiment."—*Willard Phillips.*   ing Post.
" Overflows with natural religion."—*Retrospective Review.*

" He has wit and humor, a lively fancy, and a style natural and
flexible, abounding in felicities of expression."—*R. W. Griswold.*

" Simple, natural, truthful; keen sense of pathos and humor."—
J. G. Whittier.
" The elements of genius are poured forth in her verses with aston-
ishing richness and prodigality."—*E. P. Whipple.*
" Talent for narration and delineation of character."—*William
Cullen Bryant.*

" Looks through external forms in search of the secret, mysterious
principles of thought, action, and being; mind in the abstract is his
constant theme."—*Alexander H. Everett.*

" Whatever comes to her from without, whether through the eye or
ear, whether in nature or art, is reflected in her writings with a halo
of beauty thrown about it by her own fancy."—*C. D. Cleveland.*

" Wrote for mankind at large; hence it is that he has earned a
fame wider than any author of modern times. The creations of his
genius shall survive through centuries to come, and only perish with
our language."—*William Cullen Bryant.*
" Has left a place in literature not easily supplied."—*W. Irving.*

" Graceful and polished style, pure taste, fine fancy, grace of deliv-
ery."—*Cleveland.*
" Vivid feeling and fancy."—*Leigh Hunt.*

" On the arena of metaphysics he stood the highest of all his contemporaries; and we know not what most to admire in him, whether
the deep philosophy that issued from his pen, or the humble or child-
like piety that issued from his pulpit."—*Dr. Chalmers.*

" Sui generis; vague nobleness and thorough sweetness; conquers
minds as well as hearts wherever he goes, and, without convincing
anybody's reason of any one thing, exalts their reason, and makes
it better worth having."—*Harriet Martineau.*

AUTHOR.	CLASS.	FORM.	REPRESENTATIVE WORKS.
12. EVERETT, EDWARD 1794–1865.	Rhetorician.	Tale. Oration.	Dirge of Alaric. · *Phi Beta Kappa Oration.*
13. FRANKLIN, BENJAMIN 1706–1790.	Physicist.	Essay. Letter. History.	*Letters and Papers on Electricity. Essays on General Politics, Economy, and Commerce. Essays on Religious and Moral Subjects, and the Economy of Life. Tracts Historical and Political.* *Correspondence.* *Autobiography.*
14. GILES, HENRY 1819–	Sentimentalist.	Lecture.	*Illustrations of Genius in some of its Relations to Culture and Society.*
15. HALLECK, FITZ-GREENE 1795–1869.	Sentimentalist.	Tale.	Fanny. Burns. Marco Bozzaris.
16. HAMILTON, ALEXANDER 1757–1804.	Critic.	Essay.	*The Federalist. Papers by Camillus, and Pacificus.*
17. HAWTHORNE, NATH'L 1805–1864.	Metaphysician.	Tale. Narration.	*Tanglewood Tales. Mosses from an Old Manse. Twice-told Tales.* *House of the Seven Gables. The Scarlet Letter. Marble Faun.*
18. HILDRETH, RICHARD 1807–1865.	Sentimentalist.	Essay. Treatise. History.	*Contributions to Review.* *Theory of Politics.* *History of the United States.*
19. HILLARD, GEORGE S. 1808–	Critic.	Essay.	*Six Months in Italy.* *Series of Readers.*

"Style rich and glowing, but always under the command of good taste and sound judgment. Inspiration of a generous and comprehensive patriotism."—*George S. Hillard.*

"A singular felicity of induction guided all his researches, and by very small means he established very grave truths."—*Sir Humphrey Davy.*

"His genius ranks him with the Galileos and Newtons of the old world."—*Lord Brougham.*

"Soundness, sagacity, quickness of penetration, and lively imagination. Style has the vigor and conciseness of Swift, without his harshness."—*Francis Jeffrey.*

"Franklin was the greatest diplomatist of the eighteenth century. He never spoke a word too soon; he never spoke a word too late; he never spoke a word too much; he never failed to speak the right word in the right place."—*George Bancroft.*

"Works of merit."—*American Cyclopædia*, 1869

"Poor Richard's Almanac" was one of the most influential books that ever issued from the American press.

"Pervading grace, natural brilliancy of wit, freedom, yet refinement of sentiment, sparkling flow of fancy, power of personification blended with high finish and exquisite nicety of taste."—*R. W. Griswold.*

"Master of metrical harmony."—*W. C. Bryant.*

"The Federalist derives its weight and power from Hamilton."—*George T. Curtis.*

"Superior comprehensiveness, practicalness, and originality; condensed and polished diction."—*R. W. Griswold.*

"Knows the vital principles and fundamental conditions of government."—*Guizot.*

"Model of eloquence and fascinating orator."—*Judge Story.*

"Style as clear as running water; external form but the representative of internal being."—*Longfellow.*

"Metaphysical or soulful; care in style, authenticity, artistic exposition; reliable as the best of Scott; resembles Balzac in analysis of human passion and consciousness; as true to humanity as Dickens."—*H. T. Tuckerman.*

"Strong and manly style, power of description and narration as an historian. The prominent qualities of his mind are courage and honesty."—*C. D. Cleveland.*

"Immense information, novel and judicious criticisms, thoughts and feelings beautifully expressed."—*Fraser's Magazine.*

"Taste fastidious; excels in arrangement and condensation; expression imaginative."—*Rufus W. Griswold.*

"Without egotism, personal or patriotic; style pointed and full of happy expressions and happy images."—*London Quarterly Review.*

"Hillard's Sixth Reader" is a remarkable collection of judicious criticisms and characteristic selections; from being a text-book, its value to the scholar is less likely to be known.

AUTHOR.	CLASS.	FORM.	REPRESENTATIVE WORKS.
20. HOFFMAN, CHARLES 1806–	Rhetorician.	Tale. Narration.	Love's Calendar. *Wild Scenes in the Forest Prairie.*
21. HOLLAND, J. G. 1819–	Sentimentalist.	Essay. Narration.	*Timothy Titcomb's Letters.* Marble Prophecy. Kathrina. Bitter- Sweet. *The Bay-Path.*
22. HOLMES, O. W. 1809–	Humorist. Satirist.	Essay. Tale. Narration.	*The Autocrat of the Breakfast-Table.* *Mechanism of Morals.* Old Ironsides. The One-Hoss Shay. *Elsie Venner.*
23. HUDSON, HENRY N. 1814–	Critic.	Treatise.	*Life, Art, and Characters of Shakespeare.* *Lectures on Shakespeare.*
24. IRVING, WASHINGTON 1783–1859.	Humorist. Sentimentalist.	Essay. Tale. Narration. History.	*Salmagundi.* *Tales of a Traveller.* Knickerbocker. N. Y. Sketch-Book. Bracebridge Hall. Wolfert's Roost. *Life of Columbus; of Washington; of* *Goldsmith.*
25. KENNEDY, JOHN P. 1795–1860.	Rhetorician.	Essay. Narration. History.	*Swallow-Barn.* *Horseshoe Robinson.* *Memoirs of the Life of William West.*
26. LONGFELLOW, H. W. 1807–	Rhetorician.	Narration. Tale. History.	*Hyperion. Kavanaugh. Outre-Mer.* Evangeline. Hiawatha. Miles Stan- dish. Excelsior. Psalm of Life. The Divine Tragedy.
27. LOWELL, JAMES RUSSELL 1819–	Humorist. Critic.	Narration. Essay.	Fable of the Critics. Agassiz. The Crisis. *Biglow Papers.* *Among My Books. My Study Win-* *dows. Some of the Old Poets.*
28. MEEK, A. B. 1814–1865.	Sentimentalist.	Tale. Narration.	Balaklava. The Red Eagle. Romantic Scenes in S. W. History.
29. MITCHELL, D. G. 1822–	Sentimentalist.	Narration.	Dream Life. Reveries of a Bachelor.

CHARACTERIZATION.

" Graphic delineations of nature, spirited sketches of men and manners, and richness and purity of style."—*Rufus W. Griswold.*

" We mean it as very high praise when we say that Bitter-Sweet is one of the few books that have found the secret of drawing up and assimilating the juices of this new world of ours."—*Atlantic Monthly.*

Under the editorial management of Dr. Holland the Springfield Republican made the reputation which it has so long and so well deserved.

"Most concise, apt, and effective poet of the school of Pope."—*H. T. Tuckerman.*

" Mr. Hudson has enriched the literature of our language with the fruits of his studies, mastering the difficulties of the poet with wonderful ingenuity, seizing the spirit of his characterization with kindred subtlety, and in a singularly nervous and racy style presenting some of the finest specimens of critical analysis of which any modern writer can boast."—*S. Austen Allibone.*

" Rich and original humor, great refinement of feeling and delicacy of sentiment. Style accurately finished, easy, and transparent. Accurate observer: his descriptions are correct, animated, and beautiful."—*George S. Hillard.*

" Altogether one of our most genial, lively, and agreeable writers. His style is airy, easy, and graceful, but various, and always in keeping with his subject. He excels both as a describer and as a raconteur."—*R. A. Griswold.*

" Affluence of imagination."—*E. P. Whipple.*
" Purity of tone, tenderness, picturesque simplicity."—*James Russell Lowell.*
" His poetry expresses a universal sentiment in the simplest and most melodious manner."—*George W. Curtis.*
" Beauty of imagination, delicacy of taste, wide sympathy, and mild earnestness."—*George Gilfillan.*

Poets and Poetry of Europe. Translation of Dante.

" Conception superior to execution ; imagination vivid, and fancy fruitful ; purity and elevation of feeling."—*George S. Hillard.*

Throughout My Study Windows are scattered some of our most judicious art criticisms. Mr. Lowell always writes effectively, but is sometimes reproached with want of elegance in language and structure.

" The poetry of A. B. Meek is marked by exquisite melody of versification, great delicacy of sentiment, and a manliness of feeling rarely met with."—*South.Lit. Mess. Dec.* 1857.

Meek's poem of Balaklava was published under an assumed name.

" Prose graphic and musical, poetical in spirit, and characterized by purity as well as tenderness of feeling."—*George S. Hillard.*

AUTHOR.	CLASS.	FORM.	REPRESENTATIVE WORKS.
30. MORRIS, GEORGE P. 1802–1864.	Sentimentalist.	Tale.	Woodman, spare that Tree.
31. MOTLEY, JNO. LOTHROP 1814–	Rhetorician.	History.	*History of the United Netherlands. Rise of the Dutch Republic. Life and Times of John Barneveldt.*
32. PARKER, THEODORE 1812–1860.	Sentimentalist.	Essay. Address. Tale	*Critical and Miscellaneous Writings. Sermons.* Poems.
33. PARSONS, T. W. 1819–	Rhetorician.	Tale.	Poems.
34. PAULDING, JAMES K. 1778–1860.	Humorist. Satirist.	Essay. Narration.	*Salmagundi. John Bull and Brother Jonathan.*
35. PHILLIPS, WENDELL 1811–	Sentimentalist.	Oration. Essay.	*Antislavery Orations. The Lost Arts.*
36. PIERPONT, JOHN 1785–1866.	Sentimentalist.	Tale.	Airs of Palestine. Series of Readers.
37. POE, EDGAR ALLAN 1819–1849.	Rhetorician.	Tale.	Annabel Lee. The Raven. *Prose Tales.*
38. PRENTICE, GEORGE D. 1802–1869.	Humorist.	Essay. Tale.	*Editorials. Prenticeiana.* The Tempest.
39. PRESCOTT, WILLIAM H. 1796–1859.	Rhetorician.	Essay. History.	*Biographical and Critical Miscellanies. Ferdinand and Isabella. Conquest of Mexico; of Peru. Philip II.*

CHARACTERIZATION.

"Best American song-writer."—*T. B. Shaw.*

REMARKS.

Together with N. P. Willis, Morris published "The Prose and Poetry of Europe and America."

"Style always copious, occasionally familiar, sometimes stilted and declamatory."—*Guizot.*

"Research and accuracy."—*W. H. Prescott.*

"Brilliant style, generous in tone, penetrated with the true philosophy of history."—*George S. Hillard.*

"Fitness to reach the heart of mankind, and to feed its inmost longings."—*John Weiss.*

Theodore Parker was an iconoclast, and his services must be judged from this standpoint.

"His verses are clear alike to the ear and the brain, and their old-fashioned music is in keeping with their vigorous sense, fine humor, sharp but not ungenial wit, and delicate though always manly sentiment."—*R. W. Griswold.*

Translator of Dante.

"Every style of the facetious and satirical; more whimsical than Irving, less refined. Descriptive power, skill in character-writing, natural humor."—*Rufus W. Griswold.*

"Perfectly easy, quiet, almost conversational style; thoroughly prepared, he speaks as if extemporaneously; most polished sentences, most brilliant epigrams, most withering sarcasms; his intellectual bitterness is coated with honey."

"Imagine how many men and women now living first learned to love beautiful prose and finished verse through early familiarity with Pierpont's First Class Book."—*H. T. Tuckerman.*

"Fictions as matter-of-fact as De Foe; tales as weird and wonderful as Hoffman; amatory strains trembling with passion and suffused with the purple glow of love. Dirges express the dreariest essence of desolation."—*George Gilfillan.*

"Three fifths genius and two fifths fudge."—*James Russell Lowell.*

"Heart squeezed out by the mind."—*Idem.*

"The Prenticeiana are famous: . . . . an instructive and amusing commentary on the management of elections, newspaper literature, and political oratory."—*Allibone.*

"Excellent history."—*Henry Hallam.*

"An enduring history."—*Von Humboldt.*

"A classic in our language."—*George S. Hillard.*

"Faultless lucidity."—*George Bancroft.*

"Talents artistic rather than philosophical; skillful narrative and graceful style."—*H. T. Tuckerman.*

AUTHOR.	CLASS.	FORM.	REPRESENTATIVE WORKS.
40. REED, HENRY 1808–1854.	Sentimentalist.	Lecture.	*Lectures on English Literature. Lectures on History as illustrated by Shakespeare.*
41. SARGENT, EPES 1814–	Sentimentalist.	Tale. History.	Songs of the Sea. Velasco : a Tragedy. *Life and Services of Henry Clay. Series of Readers.*
42 SAXE, JOHN G. 1816–	Humorist. Satirist.	Narration. Tale.	The Money King. The Times. Progress. Rape of the Lock. Humorous and Satirical Poems.
43. SEDGEWICK, CATH. M. 1789–1867.	Sentimentalist.	Tale. Narration.	*Stories for Young Persons. Tales and Sketches of Home. Hope Leslie. Poor Rich Man, and Rich Poor Man.*
44. SIGOURNEY, LYDIA H. 1791–1865.	Sentimentalist.	Tale. Essay.	*Tales and Essays for Children. Moral Pieces in Prose and Verse. Letters to Young Ladies.*
45. SPARKS, JARED 1794–1866.	Sentimentalist.	History.	*The Diplomatic Correspondence of the American Revolution. The Writings of George Washington. The Library of American Biography. Life of Benjamin Franklin.*
46. STOWE, HARRIET B. 1812–	Sentimentalist.	Essay. Narration.	*Little Foxes. Queer Little People. House and Home Papers. Uncle Tom's Cabin. Dred. Oldtown Folks. Minister's Wooing.*
47. TAYLOR, BAYARD 1825–	Rhetorician.	Tale. Narration. Essay.	Ximena. Rhymes of Travel. *Eldorado. Land of the Saracens. At Home and Abroad. Visit to China. India and Japan.*
48. TICKNOR, GEORGE T. 1791–	Critic.	History. Essay.	*History of Spanish Literature. Contributions to North Am. Review.*
49. TUCKERMAN, H. T. 1813–1871.	Critic.	Essay.	*Italian Sketch Book. Artist Life. Thoughts on the Poets. Essays Biographical and Critical. Characteristics of Literature.*
50. TWAIN, MARK 1835–	Humorist.	Narration.	*Innocents Abroad. Roughing It.*

CHARACTERIZATION.	*REMARKS.*

"A book full of taste, beauty, and learning."—*North Am. Review.*

"The productions of a refined and gentle mind."—*Lon. Athenæum.*

> Mr. Reed was lost in the "Arctic." His books are written by a genuine lover of literature and are among the best examples of subjective criticism.

"Worthy of the subject both in sentiment and style."—*H. T. Tuckerman.*

"He has written of the sea with more freshness and graphic power, with more true fancy and poetic feeling, than Falconer and many others of a higher reputation."—*E. P. Whipple.*

"A writer of sparkling and occasionally pungent *vers de société*, who has for many years enjoyed wide popularity in the U. S., and ought to meet with a similar reception in England."—*Lon. Athenæum.*

"Writes with uncommon elegance and purity(?) : never commonplace ; occasionally diffuse."—*W. Hillard (North Am. Review, 32).*

"Great facility in versification, fluent in thought and language, triteness and irregularity at times."—*E. P. Whipple.*

"Marshall and Sparks are very accurate."—*Washington Irving.*

"Name associated imperishably with our Revolutionary period."
—*Edward Everett.*

"Knowledge of human nature, power of description, tone of Christian morality, truthfulness to God and to humanity, richness and beauty of thought and language."—*C. D. Cleveland.*

"Highest distinction from his poetry."—*Rufus W. Griswold.*

"His prose is equable and clear, in the flowing style; the narration of a genial, healthy observer of the many manners of the world which he has seen in the most remarkable portions of its four quarters."—*Duyckinck.*

> Translation of Faust.

"Written with great conscientiousness, and with singular critical circumspection of judgment."—*F. Wolf.*

"One of the most elegant and discriminating of critics."—*Rufus W. Griswold.*

"One of the ablest essayists of any country."—*Valpareau.*

"Samuel Langhorne Clemens."

AUTHOR.	CLASS.	FORM.	REPRESENTATIVE WORKS.
51 WARE, WILLIAM 1797–1852.	Rhetorician.	Narration.	Zenobia. Julian. Probus.
52. WARNER, CHAS. DUDLEY	Humorist.	Essay.	My Summer in a Garden.
53. WAYLAND, FRANCIS 1796–1865.	Metaphysician.	Treatise. Address.	Elements of Political Economy. Elements of Moral Science. Duties of American Citizenship.
54. WEBSTER, DANIEL 1782–1852.	Sentimentalist.	Oration.	Trial of J. F. Knapp. Reply to Hayne.
55. WHIPPLE, E. P. 1819–	Rhetorician.	Essay.	Contributions to N. Am. Review. Essays and Reviews. Lectures on Subjects connected with Literature and Life. Character and Characteristic Men. Literature of the Age of Elizabeth.
56. WHITTIER, J. G. 1808–	Sentimentalist.	Tale.	Voices of Freedom. In War Times. Snow-Bound.
57. WINTHROP, THEODORE 1828–1861.	Rhetorician.	Narration. Essay.	Cecil Dreeme. John Brent. Contributions to Atlantic Monthly.
58. WIRT, WILLIAM 1772–1834.	Rhetorician.	History.	Two Principal Arguments in the Trial of Aaron Burr. Life of Patrick Henry; of Jefferson.

CHARACTERIZATION. *REMARKS.*

" Rivalled Lockhart."—*H. T. Tuckerman.*

" There is not a trace of modern habits or modes of thinking; and if Ware had been possessed by the monomania of Macpherson or Chatterton, it would have rested with himself to produce these letters as a close and literal version of manuscripts of the third century."—*Harriet Martineau.*

" Clear, exact, judicious."—*Valpareau.*

" Vigorous, logical mind; writes with clearness and energy; wide range and grasp of thought, power of intellectual construction and analysis."—*George S. Hillard.*

" Stringent, terse, simple, strong."—*Chancellor Kent.*

" High standard of truth; convince him and he cannot reply; he cannot look the truth in the face and oppose it by argument."—*John C. Calhoun.*

" None of our critics is more successful in illustrating truth or in producing a fair and distinct impression of an author."—*Rufus W. Griswold.*

" Fineness of perception, independence of judgment, and undeviating regard for the true interests of intelligence."—*G. Valpareau.*

" Earnestness of tone, high moral purpose, energy of expression, spirit of a sincere and fearless reformer, themes drawn largely from the history, traditions, manners, and scenery of New England. Describes natural scenery correctly and beautifully, and has a vein of tenderness."—*George S. Hillard.*

" Displays a wonderful power of imagination."—*Trübner.* Killed at Great Bethel.

" I do not think highly of his literary merits; abilities more brilliant than solid, rapid but skillful command of language, prolific but not chaste or correct fancy; opinions neither new nor striking."—*Rufus W. Griswold.*

" Style polished and forcible."—*Trübner.*

Wirt's " Blind Preacher " has entranced thousands of young people, and is a masterpiece of descriptive writing.

AUTHOR.	WORKS.	REASON FOR MENTION.
1. ADAMS, JOHN 1735–1826.	Works.	"The great pillar of support to the Declaration of Independence, and its ablest advocate and champion on the floor of the House, was John Adams."—*Thomas Jefferson.*
2. ADAMS, J. Q. 1767–1848.	*Eulogies on Monroe, Madison, and Lafayette.*	A statesman of world-wide reputation.
3. AGASSIZ, LOUIS J. R. 1807–1873.	*Contributions to Natural History of U. S.*	Leading naturalist.
4. ALCOTT, A. BRONSON 1799–	*Tablets.*	"The Orphic Sage." Celebrated conversationist.
5. ALCOTT, LOUISA M. 1833–	*Little Women*	The best-known author of juvenile literature.
6. ANTHON, CHARLES 1797–1867.	*Editions of the Classics.*	Known to all American students as a classical scholar.
7. AUDUBON, JOHN J. 1782–1851.	*Birds of America. Quadrupeds of America.*	Leading ornithologist.
8. BEECHER, H. W. 1813–	*Star-Papers.* *Lectures to Young Men.*	Perhaps the best known of American pulpit orators.
9. BURRITT, ELIHU 1811–	*Mission of Great Suffering.*	Known as the "Learned Blacksmith," and celebrated for the number of languages with which he is acquainted.
10. BUSHNELL, HORACE C. 1804–	*Nature and the Supernatural, as together constituting the one System of God.*	Celebrated theologian.
11. CALHOUN, JOHN C. 1782–1850.	*Works.*	Praised by Daniel Webster for the closeness of his logic; identified with national history for forty years.
12. CAREY, HENRY C. 1793–	*Principles of Social Science.*	"Among the very first of political economists."—*C. D. Cleveland.*
13. CHEEVER, GEORGE B. 1807–	*American Commonplace Book of Prose. Studies in Poetry,* with Biographical Sketches of the Poets.	"Evinces genius, scholarship, and industry in an eminent degree."—*C. D. Cleveland.*
14. CHOATE, RUFUS 1799–1859.	*Orations.*	Distinguished advocate.
15. CLAY, HENRY 1777–1852.	*Speeches.*	Distinguished orator and statesman.

	AUTHOR.	WORKS.	REASON FOR MENTION.
16.	COZZENS, FRED S. 1818-1869.	Sparrowgrass Papers.	One of the most delicate of our humorists.
17.	DANA, JAMES D. 1813-	Mineralogy. Geology.	Leading physicist.
18.	DANA, R. H., Sr. 1787-	The Buccaneer.	Editor of North American Review, and one of the first to give reputation to its literary criticisms.
19.	DANA, R. H., Jr. 1815-	Two Years before the Mast.	Success of the venture.
20.	DRAPER, JOHN WILLIAM 1811-	Physiology. Intellectual Development of Europe.	Leading physiologist.
21.	DWIGHT, TIMOTHY 1752-1847.	System of Divinity.	Well known as a theologian and as president of Yale College.
22.	EVERETT, ALEXANDER H. 1790-1847.	Critical and Miscellaneous Essays.	Editor of North American Review, and pronounced by Cleveland "one of the most eminent literary men of our country."
23.	FLINT, TIMOTHY 1780-1840.	Recollections of Ten Years passed in the Valley of the Mississippi.	"First important contribution to American geography."—C. D. Cleveland.
24.	FULLER, MARGARET 1810-1850.	Woman in the Nineteenth Century. At Home and Abroad.	Known also as Marchesa d'Ossoli. Celebrated as a conversationist. Lost at sea.
25.	GOODRICH, SAMUEL G. 1793-1860.	Thirty-Six Volumes of Tales.	"Peter Parley." Published The Token, our first annual.
26.	GRAY, ASA 1810-	Manual of Botany.	Leading botanist.
27.	GRISWOLD, RUFUS W. 1815-1857.	Poets and Poetry of America. Prose Writers of America. Female Poets of America.	Represents with Duyckinck our American anthology.
28.	HEDGE, F. H. 1805-	Prose Writers of Germany.	Best collected translations from the German.
29.	HOPKINS, MARK 1802-	Lectures on the Evidences of Christianity. The Law of Love, and Love as Law.	One of the best loved and most esteemed of college presidents; known throughout America by his teachings.
30.	HOPKINSON, FRANCIS 1737-1791.	The New Roof.	Signer of Declaration of Independence; well known as an agreeable satirist.

AUTHOR.	WORKS.	REASON FOR MENTION.
31. JEFFERSON, THOMAS 1743–1826.	Manual of Parliamentary Practice. Declaration of Independence.	Influence upon American statesmanship.
32. MADISON, JAMES 1751–1836.	Papers in the Federalist. Debates in Constitutional Convention.	Able statesman of the Revolutionary period.
33. MANN, HORACE 1796–1859.	Speeches and Lectures on Education.	Leader in public education.
34. MARCH, F. A.	Anglo-Saxon Reader and Grammar.	Eminent philologist.
35. MARSH, GEORGE P. 1801–	Origin and History of English Language. Lectures on English Language and Literature.	Eminent philologist.
36. PORTER, NOAH 1811–	The Human Intellect.	Well known as president of Yale College.
37. ROBINSON, EDWARD 1794–1863.	Palestine, Past and Present.	Founder of the "Bibliotheca Sacra."
38. SCHOOLCRAFT, HENRY 1793–1864.	Journal of Travels.	Eminent archæologist.
39. SEWARD, WILLIAM H. 1801–1872.	Travels around the World.	Long identified with the political history of the U. S.
40. STEPHENS, ALEX. H. 1812–	History of the War between the States.	For the value of the constitutional résumé in his first volume.
41. STORY, JOSEPH 1779–1845.	Commentaries on the Constitution of U. S. Lectures on Science of Government.	Leading jurist.
42. SUMNER, CHARLES 1811–1874.	The Scholar, Artist, Philanthropist, Jurist.	Succeeded Daniel Webster in the U. S. Senate, and distinguished himself as one of the most learned of that body ; as representative of the Antislavery movement his name is historical.
43. THOREAU, H. D. 1817–1862.	A Week on Concord and Merrimac Rivers. Walden. Maine Woods.	Lover of inanimate nature ; the American Rousseau.
44. VERPLANCK, GULIAN C. 1781–1870.	Procès Verbal. Editions of Shakespeare.	Leading American Shakespearean scholar.
45. WEISS, JOHN 1818–	Life and Correspondence of Theodore Parker.	Leading contributor to N. Am. Review.

AUTHOR.	WORKS.	REASON FOR MENTION.
46 WEBSTER, NOAH 1758–1843.	*Spelling Book. Dictionary.*	Still the standard lexicographer, although the dictionary leaves much to be desired.
47. WHITE, RICHARD GRANT 1812–	*Editions of Shakespeare.*	Leading American Shakespearean textual critic.
48. WILKES, CHARLES 1805–	*Cruise of the U. S. Exploring Expedition.*	"Does both himself and his country much honor."—*London Athenæum.*
49. WITHERSPOON, JOHN 1722–1794.	*Essay on Money as a Medium of Commerce.*	"One of the most influential statesmen and scholars of the Revolutionary period."—*C. D. Cleveland.*
50. WOOLMAN, JOHN 1720–1772.	*Works.*	"Get the writings of Woolman by heart, and love the early Quakers." —*Charles Lamb.*
51. WOOLSEY, T. D. 1801–	*Greek Classics.*	Greek scholar, and president of Yale College for more than a quarter of a century.
52. WOODWORTH, SAMUEL 1785–1812.	The Old Oaken Bucket.	Universally known song.
53. WORCESTER, J. E. 1784–1865.	*Dictionary. Gazetteer.*	Divides with Noah Webster popular suffrage

www.ingramcontent.com/pod-product-compliance
Lightning Source LLC
Chambersburg PA
CBHW022204020726
47496CB00008B/2872